KRAKEN ME UP

JEFFREY EBBELER

I Like to Read®
COMICS ™

HOLIDAY HOUSE · NEW YORK

D0962124

That is when I saw it in the water.

It was ink.
Kraken ink.

At first he was scared.

If they are
scared of
you . . .

Yuck! Kraken ink.

. . . find a way to make them smile.

DIP

I told you they eat ships.

FOR MY DAUGHTER ISABEL,
WHOM I'M SURE WOULD LOVE
TO HAVE A PET KRAKEN

I Like to Read® Comics instill confidence and the joy of reading in new readers.
Created by award-winning artists as well as talented newcomers, these imaginative books
support beginners' reading comprehension with extensive visual support.

We hope that all new readers will say, "I like to read comics!"

Visit our website for flash cards, activities, and more about the I Like to Read® series:
www.holidayhouse.com/ILiketoRead
#ILTR

I LIKE TO READ is a registered trademark of Holiday House Publishing, Inc.

HOLIDAY HOUSE is registered in the U.S. Patent and Trademark Office.
Printed and bound in May 2021 at C&C Offset, Shenzhen, China.
The artwork was made digitally on an iPad with Procreate.
www.holidayhouse.com
First Edition
1 3 5 7 9 10 8 6 4 2

Library of Congress Cataloging-in-Publication Data
Names: Ebbeler, Jeffrey, author, illustrator.
Title: Kraken me up / Jeff Ebbeler.
Description: First edition. | New York : Holiday House, [2021] | Series:
I like to read comics | Audience: Ages 4-8 | Audience: Grades 2-3
Summary: When Izzie brings her pet Kraken to the county fair everyone
thinks he is frightening, but he is like Izzie, sweet and shy, and
Kraken and Izzie use creativity and humor to win over the crowd.
Identifiers: LCCN 2021013010 | ISBN 9780823450176 (hardcover)
Subjects: LCSH: Graphic novels. | CYAC: Graphic novels. | Kraken—Fiction.
Pets—Fiction. | Humorous stories.
Classification: LCC PZ7.7.E25 Kr 2021 | DDC 741.5/973—dc23
LC record available at https://lccn.loc.gov/2021013010

ISBN: 978-0-8234-5017-6 (hardcover)